Karen's Spy Mystery

Little Sister

Karen's Spy Mystery
Ann M. Martin

Illustrations by Susan Crocca Tang

A
LITTLE APPLE
PAPERBACK

SCHOLASTIC INC.
New York Toronto London Auckland Sydney
Mexico City New Delhi Hong Kong

No part of this publication may be reproduced in whole or in part, or stored in a retrieval system, or transmitted in any form or by any means, electronic, mechanical, photocopying, recording, or otherwise, without written permission of the publisher. For information regarding permission, write to Scholastic Inc., Attention: Permissions Department, 555 Broadway, New York, NY 10012.

ISBN 0-590-52356-2

12 11 10 9 8 7 6 5 4 3 2 1   9/9 0 1 2 3 4/0

Printed in the U.S.A.   40
First Scholastic printing, July 1999

The author gratefully acknowledges
Diane Molleson
for her help
with this book.

Karen's Spy Mystery

Downtown Stoneybrook

"It does so look like a tree," my brother Andrew said. He held up his drawing so Nancy and I could see it better. "See, this part is the trunk." Andrew pointed to some squiggly black lines. "And this is the tree." Andrew put his thumb on the green and red scribbles. My brother Andrew is four going on five. I am seven. And my name is Karen Brewer.

"What is the red for?" Nancy asked. Nancy Dawes is one of my best friends.

"Those are apples growing on my tree," Andrew answered proudly.

"Oh," said Nancy. She was quiet after that. So was I. I did not want to hurt Andrew's feelings.

We were drawing at the dining room table because it is the biggest table in the little house. (I have two houses, a big one and a little one. I will tell you more about them in awhile.)

We were inside because it was too hot to play in the yard. It was July — the hottest month of the year.

"Would you like a snack?" Mommy called from the kitchen, where she was making lemonade.

"Sure," I replied. Andrew nodded. Nancy grinned. Mommy is usually at work during the day. But she had to take the afternoon off because Merry, our nanny, needed to go to the dentist.

Soon Mommy came into the dining room with a big pitcher of lemonade, a plate of cookies, and four glasses. The glasses were full of ice. Thank goodness. It was hot even in the house.

Mommy poured the lemonade, then went back into the kitchen. She said she had to make a phone call.

I drank two glasses of lemonade. Then I felt better. "You know what I am doing this summer?" I asked, waving my half-eaten cookie in the air.

Nancy looked at me. "What?"

Andrew did not even look up. He was too busy eating. He already knew my news anyway.

"I have a job helping Mommy," I said proudly.

"You do?" Nancy's eyes were wide.

"Yes, I am going to be polishing and wrapping bracelets," I announced. (Mommy works in a crafts center making the most beautiful jewelry.) "She has a big project that she has to finish by the end of this month."

"And Mommy is paying her," Andrew added. Andrew was very impressed with my job. He was also a little upset he could not work for Mommy.

Mommy walked back into the dining room. "Can't I work for you too?" Andrew asked. He had been asking Mommy that question a lot, ever since Mommy had told me about my job the night before.

"You can when you are older," answered Mommy.

Andrew did not look too happy.

"What will you do with all the money you make?" Nancy asked me. "Do you think you should open a bank account?"

Nancy's father is the president of a big bank in town. That is probably why she thought of that. I had been thinking of putting the money in my piggy bank. But a bank account sounded much more grown-up.

"What an excellent idea," said Mommy. "What do you think, Karen?"

"Would a bank account be better than my piggy bank?"

"Much better." Nancy sounded very sure about this. "Your money would be safer."

"I guess so," I said. "Would it be my very own account?"

"Yes, we could open an account in your name," said Mommy.

"Can we do it now?" I wanted to know. "At Nancy's father's bank?"

Mommy laughed. "We should wait for Seth." (Seth is my stepfather.) "When he comes home, we can all go downtown together and have dinner afterward to celebrate. You can come with us too, Nancy. The bank is open late tonight."

"Yes!" I shouted. I did not think I could wait for Seth. But it turned out I had a lot to do to get ready. Nancy told me I would need some money to open my account. We went up to my room and took some quarters out of my piggy bank. Then we sharpened some pencils and put them in my backpack because Nancy said I would need to fill out some forms.

Before long, we were in the car on our way to the Stoneybrook Savings Bank. Nancy could not come with us because her mother needed her at home. But before she left, I thanked her for her great idea.

Stoneybrook Savings Bank is in a big, gray building. Andrew and I usually like to chase each other around the huge lobby. But today I decided we should act more grown-up. I tried to be patient while we waited in line. When it was finally our turn, Mommy and Seth did most of the talking. Boo and bullfrogs!

The lady helping us was named Cynthia. She told me she was a personal banker — *my* personal banker. She gave me some forms to fill out. I took out my pencils, but Cynthia told me I should write in pen. I was signing my name very carefully when Mr. Dawes walked by. He waved when he saw me and said, "Hello, Karen."

"You know Mr. Dawes?" asked Cynthia.

"Oh, yes," I said.

Cynthia looked impressed. I handed the forms back to her and stood up very straight. I now had my own bank account. And the president of the bank had talked to me!

"Now can we eat?" asked Andrew.

"Sure," said Seth. "Where would you like to go?"

"Pizza Express!" we cried. Andrew and I are always in the mood for pizza.

We ordered the special with lots of pepperoni and cheese. I sank into the soft leather booth. I felt like a Very Happy — and Very Important — Person.

My Little House

We stayed at Pizza Express for a long time. It was almost dark when we came home, but Mommy had left some lights on in the little house. As we drove up the driveway, I could see into my room. My stuffed cat, Goosie, was on my bed. My favorite drawings hung over my desk. Clothes and books were everywhere. My little-house room looked a little messy. But, you know, my big-house bedroom always looks a little messy too.

I think it is time for me to tell you about my two houses.

First of all, I did not always live in two houses. When I was very little, Andrew and I lived in the big house with Mommy and Daddy here in Stoneybrook, Connecticut. Then Mommy and Daddy began fighting — at first a little, and then a lot. Finally they got a divorce. (That means they are not married to each other anymore.) Mommy, Andrew, and I moved out of the big house to a little house. That is the house I am in now. Daddy stayed at the big house. After all, it is the house he grew up in.

Then Mommy married Seth Engle. Now he is my stepfather. He came to live with us in the little house. And he brought his cat, Midgie, and his dog, Rocky, with him.

Then Daddy married a woman named Elizabeth Thomas. That made Elizabeth my stepmother. Elizabeth and all her children came to live with Daddy in the big house. Her children are Sam and Charlie, who are so old they go to high school; Kristy, who is thirteen and the best stepsister ever; and David Michael, who is seven like me. They are my stepbrothers and stepsister.

Then Daddy and Elizabeth adopted Emily Michelle from a country called Vietnam. Emily is two and a half. (I love her so much that I named my pet rat after her.)

There were so many people at the big house that Nannie, Elizabeth's mother, moved in to help take care of everyone. Nannie also helps out with the pets. There is a puppy named Shannon, a kitten named Pumpkin, our fish, Andrew's pet hermit crab, and my rat, Emily Junior.

Andrew and I spend every other month with Mommy in the little house. We live with Daddy during the other months.

I made up special nicknames for Andrew and me. I call us Andrew Two-Two and Karen Two-Two. (I thought up those names after my teacher read a book to our class. It was called *Jacob Two-Two Meets the Hooded*

Fang.) Andrew and I are two-twos because we have two of so many things. We have two houses, two families, two mommies, two daddies, two cats, and two dogs. Plus I have two stuffed cats who look exactly alike. Goosie lives at the little house. Moosie stays at the big house. I even have two pairs of glasses. The blue ones are for reading. The pink ones are for the rest of the time. Andrew and I have two sets of clothes, books, and toys. This way, we do not need to pack much when we go back and forth.

I even have a best friend near each house. Nancy lives next door to Mommy. Hannie Papadakis lives across the street and one house down from Daddy. Nancy, Hannie, and I call ourselves the Three Musketeers because we do everything together. We are even in the same class at school. (But we do not have school now because it is July.)

The door to my little house is painted red. As soon as Seth unlocked it, I could hear the phone ringing. Mommy ran to answer it.

"Karen, it's for you," Mommy called.

For me? Who was calling this late? Could it be someone calling about my bank account? I raced to the phone.

"It is Nancy," Mommy told me. "She says she has something very important to tell you."

Nancy's News

"Karen, guess what," Nancy said when I picked up the phone.

"What?"

Nancy did not say anything for a long time. "What?" I repeated.

"I am going away," Nancy finally said.

"You are?" (This was a surprise.) "Where are you going?"

"To Seattle." Nancy sounded excited.

"Seattle? That is on the other side of the country."

"Yes. My dad has to go there for business,

and he is taking us. We will stay in Seattle for ten days, then maybe go camping in the mountains."

"How long will you be gone?"

"Two weeks."

"Two weeks!" I shrieked. That seemed like forever.

"I promise I will send letters and postcards," Nancy said. "I will tell you everything I am doing."

"I will write too," I promised. (I am very good about writing letters. I write to Maxie, my pen pal in New York, and to my grandmother in Nebraska.) Still, that was not the same as having Nancy around.

"Does Hannie know?" I asked.

"Yes. She was a little upset too."

"Of course she was. We do everything together."

"I know," Nancy said. She sounded sort of sad too. Then Nancy reminded me that I had been gone a long time when I went to Chicago.

"That is true," I said. (I went to Chicago

15

when Mommy, Seth, and Andrew moved there because of Seth's work. They were there six months, but I came home after only a month. I was *very* homesick.)

"Anyway, Karen, when you came back, we were still best friends. Nothing changed."

"I know nothing will change," I said.

"My parents are looking for someone to take care of the house while we are gone." Nancy seemed to want to change the subject. "They will pay someone to live here."

"Really?"

"Well, someone is going to have to water all of my mother's plants, mow the lawn, and repair anything that breaks while we are gone."

"Hmmm," I said to show Nancy I was listening. I was getting a brilliant idea.

"The house-sitter will also have to take out the garbage and the recycling," Nancy added.

"Taking out the garbage is my job at home," I said. "I am also very good at weeding." I said this hoping Nancy would tell me that I would be a great house-sitter. But she did not. Instead she started talking about what she should pack.

I interrupted. "Nancy," I began, "I think I would be a perfect house-sitter."

Nancy did not say anything, so I kept talking. "I live right next door. I can watch your house and make sure nothing happens to it."

"That is true," said Nancy. She did not sound too sure, though. So I went on to tell Nancy how Seth could help me fix things around her house. (I had not talked to Seth about this. But I was sure he would help me.)

Before we hung up, Nancy said she would ask her parents if I could be their house-sitter. I really hoped they would say yes.

"I know I cannot live by myself in Nancy's house," I said to Mommy when she was tucking me in for the night. "But I live next door. I can be just as responsible as someone who is living there."

"I suppose you could," said Mommy. She bent down to kiss me good night.

"Besides," I said, "I could put the money I earn into my new bank account."

Mommy laughed.

Pokey

The next day, Saturday, I woke up early. I wanted to go over to Nancy's house right away. But I had to eat breakfast first. Then I had to get dressed. Who would hire a house-sitter dressed in pajamas and fuzzy pink slippers?

I thought very hard about what I should wear. I wanted Nancy's parents to think I was grown-up and responsible. I found my turquoise party dress on the floor of my closet. It was a little wrinkled, but I put it on anyway. My white tights were behind my

19

bookcase. Usually I wear tights only when it is cold. But this was a special occasion. I pulled my black patent-leather shoes from under my desk. I tied my ponytail with a turquoise bow.

"Are you going to a party?" Andrew asked when he saw me.

"No. I am applying for a job as a house-sitter next door."

"You look wonderful, Karen," said Mommy. "But you will have to be careful in those fancy clothes. And remember, Nancy's parents are not going to decide whether to hire you based on what you are wearing."

Maybe Mommy was right. I looked down at my patent-leather shoes. I did not want to scuff them. And I was already too hot in my tights.

I could change after my interview, I thought. But then I decided to change right away. I put on shorts, a T-shirt, and sandals. I felt much better. And Mommy told me I looked wonderful in my play outfit too.

"Hello, Karen," said Nancy when she answered the door.

"Did you talk to your parents?" I asked. I could not wait to find out if I had the job.

"Yes. They want to see you," Nancy answered. I followed Nancy to her family room. Mr. Dawes sat on the couch reading the paper. Mrs. Dawes was playing with Danny, Nancy's baby brother, on the floor.

"Good morning," I said politely.

"Good morning, Karen," said Mr. Dawes. He put down his newspaper. "I hear you are wondering about the house-sitting job."

I nodded.

Mr. Dawes had some bad news. He and Mrs. Dawes said they were very sorry, but I was not the house-sitter they had in mind.

"We need an adult," Mr. Dawes explained. "You cannot live here by yourself."

"We are going away for so long, we really need someone who can mow the lawn and handle anything that goes wrong," added Nancy's mother.

"I could take care of your yard," I said. "I am very good at gardening. Mommy says so."

"I know you are, Karen," said Mrs. Dawes. "You will be an excellent house-sitter when you are old enough to stay here by yourself."

There was nothing I could say that would change their minds. I gave up trying when Mr. Dawes said he had already hired some-body else: a man named Bill Barnett, who worked at the bank. Boo and bullfrogs. I was very disappointed.

"Come on, Karen, let's play," said Nancy.

I shrugged. I did not feel like playing.

Then Nancy's mother said we could play in the study if we wanted to listen to music and dance. As soon as I heard the word *dance*, I cheered up a little.

Nancy and I spent a long time listening to our favorite CDs. And we made up our very own dances. I called my dance the shaker because I shook every part of my body. Nancy named her dance the snake because

she slithered on the floor. (I thought her dance was too hard to do.)

Then we listened to a tape of Nancy playing the clarinet. (Nancy is an excellent clarinet player. She plays in the band at school.)

"I recorded that tape myself," said Nancy proudly. She showed me the Daweses' fancy tape player. The microphone was next to the cassette player. "You just put in a blank tape, set this knob to 'microphone,' " said Nancy, "and press 'record' and 'play' at the same time."

"Cool," I said. "Let's make a tape of ourselves singing 'Sisters.' " So we did.

After lunch Mr. Dawes said we could play with some brand-new software on his computer. I used it to design a cool poster. It showed two ballerinas dancing. "One is doing the snake, the other the shaker," I said.

Nancy laughed. She loved my poster and wanted to print it. But we did not know how. Nancy told me that we could not play around with the computer trying to find out how to print because her dad uses it for work. "Did you know that my father can look in his files at the bank?"

"With this computer?" I asked.

Nancy nodded. "He can go to work without leaving our house!"

"Can anyone get into the bank's files?" I asked. I was worried about my brand-new account.

"Oh, no," Nancy answered. "You need a secret password. Only my dad knows it. He will not even tell me what it is."

That was a relief.

"Nancy, it is time for Pokey to get his eyedrops," Mrs. Dawes called. (Pokey is Nancy's kitten. He is one of the most well behaved cats I know.)

"Okay," Nancy called back. Then Nancy turned to me. She looked very excited. "Karen, Pokey has an eye infection. He needs drops three times a day."

"Poor Pokey," I said.

"But he is very good about getting the drops. Anyway, Karen, thinking of Pokey just gave me a great idea."

I looked at her.

Nancy explained that the house-sitter could give Pokey his drops in the morning and evening. But someone else would have to do it in the middle of the day. And guess what? That someone could be me.

Nancy's parents agreed this was a good idea. So I discussed my salary with Nancy's mother. Then she showed me how to unlock the back door so I could let myself in and out of the house. I felt gigundoly grown-up. Now I had *two* summer jobs!

Karen Brewer:
House-sitter

"Did you pack your camera?" asked Hannie.

"And lots of paper so you can write us letters?" I asked.

"What about an umbrella?" Hannie added. "I heard it rains a lot in Seattle."

"Yes, yes, and yes," answered Nancy as she lugged her suitcase down the stairs with Hannie's help. I carried her backpack.

"Are you sure you packed enough?" Mr. Dawes joked as he loaded Nancy's suitcase into the car.

"We are going to be gone for two whole weeks," Nancy reminded her father. "And my hiking boots are heavy."

"True," Mr. Dawes agreed.

Mrs. Dawes was busy closing up the house. Danny was already in the car.

"You are going on an airplane," I said to him. "Airplane."

He cooed and smiled at me.

Mrs. Dawes came out of the house carrying a big bag stuffed with toys and snacks.

"This should keep Danny busy on the plane," she said.

"It should," I agreed. Then I cleared my throat because I had something important to tell Nancy's parents. "I will make sure your house is all right while you are away," I said. "I promise."

"I am sure you will, Karen," said Mrs. Dawes.

I nodded. (After all, I had a lot of responsibility. Bill Barnett would be away all day. And when he was at work, I was in charge.

It was a good thing I had a key to the house.)

"Good-bye, Nancy," I cried. I wrapped my arms around her, and we hugged. Then Nancy and Hannie hugged. Then all three of us hugged one another together.

"We will miss you soooo much," I said.

"I will miss you too," said Nancy. She looked as though she might cry. I felt like crying a little too. But I did not.

"I will take good care of Pokey," I promised Nancy. "And your house too."

"I know you will," said Nancy. She got in the car and buckled her seat belt.

"Good-bye, good-bye," Hannie and I shouted as the Daweses pulled away. We waved until the car was out of sight.

"What do you feel like doing now?" I asked Hannie.

"Nothing," Hannie answered. "I am too sad to do anything." We walked to my house and went inside.

Merry (our nanny) and Andrew were in

the kitchen playing with clay. Merry was making a sculpture of Andrew. It was so good, I could tell right away who it was. Andrew said he was making a cat.

"Would you like to play with us?" Andrew asked.

"No, not today," I answered.

"Would you like a snack or anything?" asked Merry.

We did not feel like eating either. Hannie and I wandered outside. We sat underneath the maple tree in the backyard and talked. I sat facing Nancy's house. I did not want anything bad to happen to it.

When Hannie left, I went to Nancy's to give Pokey his eyedrops. I had to chase him around the house a little. Finally, he jumped on Nancy's bed and curled up on her pillow. Maybe he missed her too.

"Good kitty," I said as I gave him his drops.

Pokey followed me while I checked all the rooms in Nancy's house. Everything looked just the way it was supposed to. Then I walked around the outside of the house. I made sure the windows were closed. I checked the doors to make sure they were locked. (I did not want anyone to break in.)

Then I came home, found my binoculars, and sat on a chair in my front yard, facing Nancy's house. Someone needed to watch the house during the day. If I had been chosen as the house-sitter, I would have been at the house all the time. I would have been much more responsible than Bill Barnett.

Silver and Gold

I was still sitting outside when Mommy came home from work. I told her I needed to stay outside until the other house-sitter arrived. I could not let anything happen to Nancy's house.

"Why do you need the binoculars?" asked Mommy.

"To see anything that looks suspicious."

"Karen, it is not polite to spy on people."

"I am not spying on anyone, just on the house. No one is in it," I said.

Mommy said I had to come inside for dinner when it was ready. She also told me she needed my help with jewelry-making tonight.

"Sure," I answered. (I was excited about starting my other job too.)

Soon a red car stopped in front of Nancy's house. A tall man with blond hair and a mustache stepped out. A bag was slung over his shoulder.

I figured he must be the other house-sitter. So I put down my binoculars and raced to Nancy's to introduce myself.

"Hello, I am Karen Brewer," I said. I held out my hand. "You must be Bill Barnett."

The man nodded. He was getting two suitcases out of his trunk. He did not shake my hand. "How did you know my name?" he asked.

"The Daweses told me you will be staying in their house. I am the daytime house-sitter," I said proudly.

"Oh," said Bill Barnett. He looked a little surprised.

I explained how Pokey needed eye drops

three times a day. And that it was very important to remember to give them to him, so he could get over his eye infection.

"Remind me who Pokey is."

"Pokey is the Daweses' kitten," I answered, frowning.

"Oh, that's right. I had forgotten his name. I know he needs to get eyedrops," Bill said gruffly.

I was worried. If Bill Barnett did not know who Pokey was, could he be trusted to look after a whole house?

I followed him up the steps to Nancy's front door. I watched him unlock the door and take his suitcases inside. I was hoping he would invite me in. But he did not.

"I can show you where everything is," I said. I began to follow him inside. Bill put his suitcases down and turned to face me. Then he started to close the door. "Mr. Dawes already showed me around," Bill said. "Good-bye, Karen." I decided I did not like Bill Barnett.

At dinner I told Mommy, Seth, and Andrew how unfriendly he was.

"You are not giving him much of a chance," Mommy told me.

"He slammed the front door right in my face," I said.

"It is his first night here," said Mommy. "Maybe he was tired and just wanted to get settled in peace."

"I was not bothering him at all," I huffed.

After dinner Mommy and I spread Mommy's bracelets on the dining room table. It was my job to polish each one, put it in a plastic bag, then tie the bag with a bright ribbon. I loved helping Mommy. The job was so much fun I forgot about Bill Barnett.

The bracelets were all different. Some had wide bands with designs on them. Others were in links that looked like grains of wheat. Some even had small jewels set in them. I polished the bracelets carefully so they would look their best. I put each one in its own plastic bag. Then I picked turquoise ribbon to tie the silver bracelets with, and purple and green ribbons for the gold bracelets.

When we were done for the night, Mommy put the bracelets away in a metal box with a lock on it. They needed to be kept in a safe place because they were made of gold or silver. They were very valuable.

7

The Spy Notebook

That night it was so hot that I could not sleep. I tossed and turned. I fluffed up my red pillows, shook off my sheet, then put it on again. Finally, I sat up in bed. I could see Nancy's house outside my bedroom window. The lights were still on. Maybe Bill Barnett was having trouble sleeping too.

I decided to see what he was doing. I found my binoculars on my desk. Mommy had told me it was not polite to spy on people. But I had to make sure Nancy's house was okay. After all, I promised Nancy and her parents I would look after it.

I walked to my window and focused the binoculars. The curtains in Nancy's house were open, so I could see a lot. And guess what?

Bill Barnett was in Nancy's parents' bedroom, looking at their books! Once in a while he took a book off the shelf, opened it, then put it back on the shelf. He carried a red notebook with him. Then he sat on the bed to write in it. Was he making a list of the books in Nancy's house? Was he looking for something valuable? Or maybe something to help him sleep? It was the middle of the night, after all.

Bill walked to the dresser. He picked up a vase and studied the bottom of it. Then he lifted all the pictures off the walls and turned them over to see what was on the back. How nosy!

I spent a long time watching Bill. He didn't take anything. In fact, he put everything back just where it was. Even so, I thought he was acting suspicious. What if he was planning to rob Nancy's family?

I decided I would need to spy on Bill some more no matter what Mommy said. This was too important. I would write down everything he did in a notebook. (I had kept the same kind of notebook in Chicago after someone in Mommy's apartment building was robbed. I wrote down any clue, any suspicious behavior that might help me solve the robbery. And I ended up solving it, with the help of my notes.)

I needed that notebook now. But where was it? I wasted valuable time looking for it. Who knew what Bill was up to while I searched? I finally found the notebook in the bottom drawer of my desk, buried under a pile of pink construction paper.

I flipped to a page with no writing on it. In big letters, I wrote MY SPY MYSTERY at the top. Then I took it to the window and began writing.

8

The Woman in Black

MY SPY MYSTERY
BY KAREN BREWER (DAYTIME HOUSE-SITTER
AND NIGHTTIME SPY)
OFFICIAL NOTES ON SUSPECT BILL BARNETT

TUESDAY NIGHT

I AM KEEPING THIS NOTEBOOK BECAUSE I AM
SUSPICIOUS OF BILL BARNETT, THE DAWESES'
HOUSE-SITTER.

FACTS
1) BILL ARRIVED AT NANCY'S HOUSE CARRYING
A SHOULDER BAG WITH A LAPTOP COMPUTER IN IT

AND TWO SUITCASES. (I KNOW THERE WAS A LAP-
TOP COMPUTER IN THE SHOULDER BAG BECAUSE
DADDY HAS ONE JUST LIKE IT. I DO NOT KNOW
WHAT WAS IN THE SUITCASES.)

2) BILL WAS UNFRIENDLY TO THE DAYTIME
HOUSE-SITTER (ME) AND DID NOT INVITE
HER IN THE HOUSE.

3) BILL SPENDS A LOT OF TIME IN THE
DAWESES' HOUSE LOOKING AT THEIR THINGS,
PICKING THEM UP, AND WRITING ABOUT THEM IN
A RED NOTEBOOK. HE HAS NOT CHANGED OUT OF
HIS WORK CLOTHES YET, EVEN THOUGH IT IS THE
MIDDLE OF THE NIGHT. HAS HE BEEN SNOOPING
AROUND THEIR HOUSE SINCE HE GOT THERE —
BEFORE I WAS ON THE CASE?

QUESTION: IS BILL LOOKING FOR SOMETHING?
IMPORTANT QUESTION: IS HE PLANNING A
ROBBERY?

LATER TUESDAY NIGHT

I WAS SO BUSY WRITING, I ALMOST DID NOT NO-
TICE THE BIG BLACK CAR THAT PULLED UP TO THE

42

DAWESES' HOUSE. A TALL BLONDE WOMAN GOT
OUT OF THE CAR AND RANG THE DOORBELL. BILL AN-
SWERED RIGHT AWAY AND LET HER IN. THE
WOMAN WORE A BLACK DRESS AND HIGH-HEELED
SHOES, AND HAD A LONG BLACK SCARF WRAPPED
AROUND HER NECK.

QUESTIONS: WHY IS THE WOMAN DRESSED IN
BLACK? DOES SHE WANT TO HIDE IN THE DARK?
DID SHE JUST COME FROM A FUNERAL?

THE WOMAN IN BLACK AND BILL ARE
SITTING AT THE KITCHEN TABLE. THEY HAVE
BEEN TALKING FOR A LONG TIME. I CANNOT
HEAR ANYTHING THEY ARE SAYING. BUT THIS IS
WHAT I SEE

1) BILL LOOKS HAPPY TO SEE THIS WOMAN.

2) THE WOMAN WAVES HER HANDS A LOT. SHE
POINTS TO CABINETS IN THE KITCHEN AND PANTRY

3) BILL SHAKES HIS HEAD. (I GUESS HE IS
SAYING NO, BUT I AM NOT SURE.)

QUESTION: IS THE WOMAN ASKING HIM TO ROB
THE KITCHEN? (NANCY'S FAMILY HAS REALLY NICE
CHINA IN THE CABINETS.)

4) THE WOMAN KISSES BILL GOOD-BYE BE-
FORE SHE LEAVES.

QUESTIONS: WHO WOULD WANT TO KISS BILLY? IS THIS WOMAN GOING TO HELP BILL IN THE ROBBERY?

I AM STARTING TO GET SLEEPY. MAYBE I SHOULD GO TO BED, BUT I HATE TO FALL ASLEEP BEFORE BILL DOES. BEFORE I GO TO BED, I WILL SET MY ALARM FOR 2:00 A.M. I DO NOT WANT TO MISS ANYTHING.

I AM BARELY AWAKE. SPYING IS HARD WORK. THE LIGHTS ARE STILL ON IN NANCY'S HOUSE. BILL IS STILL AWAKE. HE IS STILL IN HIS BUSINESS CLOTHES, AND HE IS SITTING IN THE KITCHEN TALKING ON THE PHONE.

QUESTIONS: WHO IS HE TALKING TO? COULD IT BE THE WOMAN IN BLACK? IS HE TELLING HER TO COME OVER TO ROB THE HOUSE? NOW WOULD BE A GOOD TIME FOR A ROBBERY BECAUSE EVERYONE IS ASLEEP. EXCEPT ME. BUT THEY DO NOT KNOW THAT. WHY IS BILL UP SO LATE, ANYWAY?

SPY KAREN BREWER IS SIGNING OFF FOR THE NIGHT.

44

P.S. NOW THAT I AM A SPY, I WILL NEED TO WEAR DARK GLASSES AND A HAT SO BILL WILL NOT RECOGNIZE ME. MAYBE A WIG TOO. BILL SHOULD NOT KNOW I SUSPECT HIM. WHAT IF HE IS DANGEROUS?

"Hannie, You Have to Believe Me!"

"You sure slept late," Andrew said to me. I sat at the kitchen table, still in my pajamas, eating a bowl of cereal. Mommy and Seth had already left for work.

"I had trouble falling asleep," I explained.

"Why?" Andrew wanted to know.

"Andrew, let Karen have her breakfast," said Merry.

I looked up at the kitchen clock. It was ten A.M. I am usually up much earlier. "I could not sleep," I said, which was true. I thought about telling Andrew and Merry about spying. But I did not. Andrew might say something to Mommy. And Merry would probably tell me not to spy on people. Besides, I needed more proof that Bill was doing something wrong. Right now, I just had proof that Bill was nosy.

"Karen, will you play with me?" asked Andrew when I finished breakfast.

"Not right now," I answered. "I have to get dressed."

"After you get dressed?" asked Andrew, following me to my bedroom.

"No, Andrew. I do not feel like playing right now." I closed my door. When I finished dressing, Andrew was still outside my door. He followed me down the hall, down the stairs, and around the house.

"Andrew, I am thinking," I said. "I need to be alone."

"Why? What are you thinking about?"

I rolled my eyes. "Andrew," I pleaded, "I need some privacy."

"Andrew, come here," Merry called at last. Thank goodness. I really did need to think.

I also needed to tell someone about Bill. Someone who would understand why I was so worried.

I called Hannie from the upstairs phone so no one could hear me. She answered on the second ring. "Hannie," I said, "you will not believe what is happening in Nancy's house."

"What?"

I told Hannie how unfriendly Bill was and how he snooped around Nancy's house, writing things in a notebook. I even told her about the woman in black. I finished by telling her Bill was still up at 2:00 A.M. talking on the phone.

"So?" said Hannie.

"So?" I repeated. "Don't you think all this makes Bill seem very suspicious? He is probably going to rob Nancy and her parents."

"Oh, Karen. Bill did not take anything, right?"

"Right," I was forced to admit. "But he was

listing practically everything in the house."

"What is wrong with that? Maybe Bill is writing a book or something."

"Hmmm," I said. I could not believe Hannie was not taking me seriously. "But what about the woman in black?"

"I am sure the Daweses did not tell Bill he could not have guests. She is probably his girlfriend."

"Hannie, you have to believe me."

"Bill has not done anything wrong."

"He was talking on the phone at two A.M. I am sure he was calling the woman in black to tell her what he stole."

"How do you know what Bill was saying? What if he was calling Nancy's family?"

"At two A.M.?"

"They are in a different time zone," Hannie reminded me. "Seattle is three hours earlier."

I sighed loudly. If Hannie did not believe me, who would?

Bill Barnett

When Hannie came over to play, I lent her my binoculars so she could spy on Bill when he came home from work. I still hoped to convince her that Bill was up to no good.

Hannie told me spying was a waste of time. And not nice, besides. But after I begged her, she finally looked through the binoculars.

"Karen, Bill is just reading a magazine," Hannie reported. "I cannot see what the title is."

"Is the family silver near him? Has he taken the china out of the cabinets?" I asked nervously.

"No, Karen. He is just sitting at the kitchen table." Hannie sounded impatient.

I sighed. Maybe Hannie was right. Maybe Bill was not a burglar. I just wished I knew for sure.

The next day, I saw Bill mowing Nancy's lawn. He had even come home early to do it. Maybe Bill was okay after all. I decided to give him another chance. I threw my Frisbee into Nancy's yard so I would have an excuse to run over there and talk to him.

This time Bill looked happy to see me. He turned off his lawn mower and picked up my Frisbee. "This must belong to you," he said as he handed it to me.

"It does," I answered politely. "Thank you." I was not sure what to say next. Luckily, Bill spoke first.

"You must be a good friend of Nancy's to

be taking such good care of her cat," he said.

"Oh, I am. Nancy and I are best friends."

"You are?" Bill sounded interested.

"Oh, yes." I went on to tell Bill how Nancy, Hannie, and I do everything together. He laughed when I told him we were the Three Musketeers.

Bill and I talked for a long time. He did not seem to want to finish mowing. In fact, he wanted to know all about Nancy: what her stuffed animals were called, what she liked to read, what songs she liked to sing. I was very proud I could answer everything. Bill was even interested in old stories about Nancy and me. "When I first met Nancy, she had a dog called Percy. We used to take him for walks."

"The dog's name was Percy?" Bill said.

"Yes. He died awhile ago. Her parents named him. Nancy told me Percy was one of the first words she learned to say."

"Really." Bill smiled. "Nancy must have been very smart."

I nodded. I could not believe how well Bill and I were getting along. Bill was not unfriendly at all.

Before I went to bed that night, I peeked out the window with my binoculars. (I could not help it.) Bill sat at the kitchen table writing in his red notebook. Nothing looked suspicious at all. Hannie was probably right. Bill had not done anything wrong.

I slept soundly knowing Nancy's house was safe.

The Junior Detective Kit

"Doesn't this bracelet look shiny?" I held it up so Andrew could see.

"I like the rock in it," said Andrew.

"That is a small ruby," I said. I had been helping Mommy most of the day. I knew all about the bracelets now.

"Can we go fly our kite?" asked Andrew.

"Andrew, it will be dark soon. We do not have time. Besides, I am working." I put the bracelet in its bag and tied it with a purple ribbon.

"Karen, you are so busy with your jobs

that you never have time to play with me anymore."

I sighed. Andrew was right. I had been very busy. "All right, Andrew, I will play with you," I said. "We can pretend the couch is a spaceship. Our stuffed animals are the crew. We will visit Mars."

Andrew beamed. He loved games like this. I must admit I liked them too. Andrew and I played until it was time to help Mommy put the bracelets away for the night. Soon it was time for Andrew to go to bed. I was allowed to stay up a little later.

I walked down the hall to the bathroom. I noticed something strange from the bathroom window. From the corner of my eye I could see a blue light shining through the blinds in Nancy's house. I did not think Nancy's family had any blue lightbulbs. This light was bright—and very mysterious.

I checked the time. It was a little after nine. That was late, but not too late to call Hannie. Not with important news like this.

Hannie did not think my news was so important. "Karen, maybe Bill is watching television," she said.

"I thought of that. But I do not think the light is coming from the TV room. This light is near the kitchen, I think."

"Maybe Bill moved the TV," Hannie suggested.

"Maybe," I said.

"Karen, why are you still so suspicious of Bill? I thought you liked him now."

"I do. I just want to be sure Nancy's house is okay. You know, I am the assistant house-sitter. I have a lot of responsibility."

I stayed up late writing in my spy notebook. When I went to bed, the blue light was still shining through the blinds. Bill must have been watching a lot of TV.

The next morning I had a plan. I decided not to tell Hannie about it because she would just laugh. My plan was to get Bill's fingerprints, in case he was a wanted criminal. It took me a long time to find my old Junior Detective Kit. I finally found it in the back of my closet. Inside was a fingerprint kit (thank goodness), a pair of spy glasses, a magnifier, a flashlight, a secret marker pen, and an agent ID card. I put on the spy glasses and carried the kit to Nancy's without Merry or Andrew seeing me. I did not want them to ask what I was doing.

When I was safely inside the house, I opened up the fingerprint kit. Inside was a jar of black powder, an ink pad, and tape. I was not sure what to do next. Luckily, there were directions on the jar.

STEP 1: Locate a fingerprint.

That would be easy. I decided to start with the kitchen. There were fingerprints on the door, the refrigerator, and the countertops. I examined them with my magnifier. The only problem was that I could not tell which ones were Bill's.

STEP 2: Sprinkle black powder over the fingerprint.

I sprinkled the black powder on the doorknob. The powder smeared everything: the

doorknob, the kitchen floor, my fingers, my clothes, even my hair.

STEP 3: Lift fingerprint with tape.

I took out the tape and dusted off some of the extra powder with my hands. Now my fingerprints were on the doorknob too. This was hopeless.

It took me a long time to clean up the mess I had made. Or maybe it seemed long because I was very worried that Bill would return. Luckily he did not. When I left Nancy's house, I had black powder in my hair and all over my clothes. But I still had no fingerprints.

And I still had no proof that Bill had done anything wrong. I did not even know if he was a wanted criminal. And now it looked as if I would never find out. Even I had to admit that.

An Important Clue

The next day I was very busy helping Mommy at the craft center. We were working there instead of at home because Mommy needed to use some equipment she doesn't have at home. Mommy worked in a big room with lots of shelves and tables. A few people sat at the tables making jewelry. I loved looking at their tools—tiny pliers and tiny clamps. Some people were even melting gold and silver over small gas burners. Everyone looked very busy.

I spent the morning polishing jewelry for

Mommy and some of her friends. Almost everyone told me how helpful I was. I felt very proud.

When it was time for lunch, I told Mommy we had to go home. Pokey needed his eyedrops.

"Pokey, where are you?" I called when I let myself into Nancy's house. Usually Pokey came to see me right away. But today he did not. I got his medicine and found him curled up on the living room rug. When I tried to pick him up, he scampered away. I chased Pokey all over the house. Finally I caught him in the study. "Got you," I said as I picked him up. Pokey purred. He even sat still when I gave him his drops.

I looked around the study. There was Mr. Dawes's computer. And then I remembered something that made me suspicious all over again. The blue glow I had seen a few nights ago had come from the study. Now that I thought about it, I was positive. The glow was from the computer, not the TV. The TV was in the next room. Why did Bill need Mr. Dawes's computer when he had his own laptop? I started to get worried. I knew Mr. Dawes could get into the bank's files with a secret password. What if Bill was breaking into the files? I had seen someone do that on a TV program. Of course, Bill would need to know the password. But no one knew it except Mr. Dawes. (I hoped.)

Even though I knew it was wrong, I decided to poke around the study. I looked at the papers on Mr. Dawes's desk. It was hard to tell what belonged to Mr. Dawes and what belonged to Bill until I found something. Under a pile of catalogs was a red notebook that looked a lot like the one I had seen Bill writing in.

I leafed through it. There were pages and pages of words and lists. I did not know what they meant. Then I saw that Bill had written down the names of Nancy's stuffed animals. How strange. Maybe he was writing a story about Nancy. I turned a page and saw the words "Open sesame." Hmm. I

knew that "Open sesame" was the secret password Ali Baba used to enter the cave of the thieves. ("Ali Baba and the Forty Thieves" is one of my favorite stories. Bill probably liked it too.)

I flipped to a new page. A slip of white paper fell out of the notebook. I picked it up. The word WITHDRAWAL was printed on the slip, followed by $1,000. Yikes. I knew withdrawal meant taking money out of the bank. How could Bill do that without the password? I flipped back a page. Was the secret password "Open sesame"? Was my account safe? I panicked and raced home to talk to Mommy. I just hoped she would listen to me.

Bill Comes to Dinner

I found Mommy eating a sandwich at the kitchen table. (Andrew and Merry were outside.) I wasted no time telling Mommy all about Bill. I even admitted that I had spied on him. Mommy frowned when I said that. But she let me keep talking. I told her I had seen him looking through the Daweses' things. And I described what I had just seen in the study.

Mommy was interested in what I had to say. She even looked a little worried when I got to the part about the withdrawal. But she told me we needed more evidence before we could accuse Bill of anything.

"I can get the red notebook," I said.

"That would not prove much," Mommy said. "The withdrawal might have come from his own account."

I had not thought of that.

"Besides," Mommy said, "it is not right to go snooping around the Daweses' house." The thing to do, Mommy said, was to get to know Bill better. "Why don't we invite him over to dinner tonight," she suggested. "I have been meaning to have him over for a meal anyway."

"I do not think that is a good idea," I said. "What if he is really a thief? We have valuable things in our house. What about the bracelets? They are made of gold and silver, you know."

But before I could stop her, Mommy called Bill and left a message for him on the Daweses' answering machine. I hoped he would not accept.

But he called when he came home to say he would be happy to join us.

I tried to convince Mommy that we should eat outside. That way, Bill would not be in the house much.

"It would be more polite to invite him inside," Mommy answered. "Besides, it looks like it might rain."

"But we are going to have a barbecue."

"I know, Karen. Seth will barbecue the chicken outside. But we will eat in the dining room." Mommy sounded firm.

I sighed. That meant I would have to watch Bill the entire evening.

I was in my room when Bill rang the doorbell. Seth let him in before I could get downstairs. But I decided Bill had not been in the house long enough to take anything yet.

"What a nice painting," Bill said to Seth. He walked to the portrait of Mommy's great-grandmother that hangs in our dining room.

"Don't touch that!" I yelped.

Bill and Seth turned to look at me. "Is anything wrong, Karen?" Seth wanted to know.

"No," I answered sheepishly.

"I was not going to touch the painting," Bill said. "I just wanted to look at it more closely."

During dinner, Bill talked mostly to Mommy and Seth. Mommy asked him a lot of questions about his work at the bank.

When Bill got up to refill his water glass in the kitchen, I followed him. I pretended I needed something in the kitchen too. Bill did not look in any of our drawers or cabinets. He could not. Not when I was standing right there.

When Bill was ready to leave, I walked with him to the closet where Seth had hung his jacket. Then I walked him to the door. Bill spent a long time thanking Seth and Mommy for dinner. I hopped on one foot, then the other. I could not wait for him to leave. I was glad when he finally did.

"Well, what did you think?" I asked Mommy.

"I thought he seemed perfectly honest," Mommy answered.

"I did too," Seth added. "He works hard, and he likes his job at the bank."

"He likes all the money in the bank," I said.

"Karen, that withdrawal slip you found could be from his account," Mommy reminded me.

I could not argue.

Dark Glasses

I decided I would just have to find out more information about Bill on my own. The only problem was, how? Then I had an idea. Mommy did not want me to snoop around the Daweses' house. But no one had said anything about spying on Bill at the bank.

The next morning, I told Merry and Andrew I needed to go downtown. "I want to deposit some money in my bank account," I said. (This was true.)

Before we left, I put on my dark spy

glasses and a straw hat. I did not want Bill to recognize me.

"I am worried about getting too much sun," I told Andrew when he asked me why I was wearing dark glasses. Merry gave me a funny look, but she did not say anything.

When we reached the bank, I stood at the end of the longest line. That way, I would have plenty of time to look around. It did not take me long to spot Bill. He was walking behind the bank tellers. And I could see everything he was doing.

I saw Bill walk to a safe and open it. I could not tell what he was doing at the safe. Maybe he was counting money.

Bill was still at the safe when it was my turn. I was so busy watching him that the bank teller had to ask me twice how she could help me.

"I want to deposit some money in my bank account," I whispered. (Even though Bill was far away, I did not want him to recognize my voice.) I handed my money to the teller. She counted it and wrote the

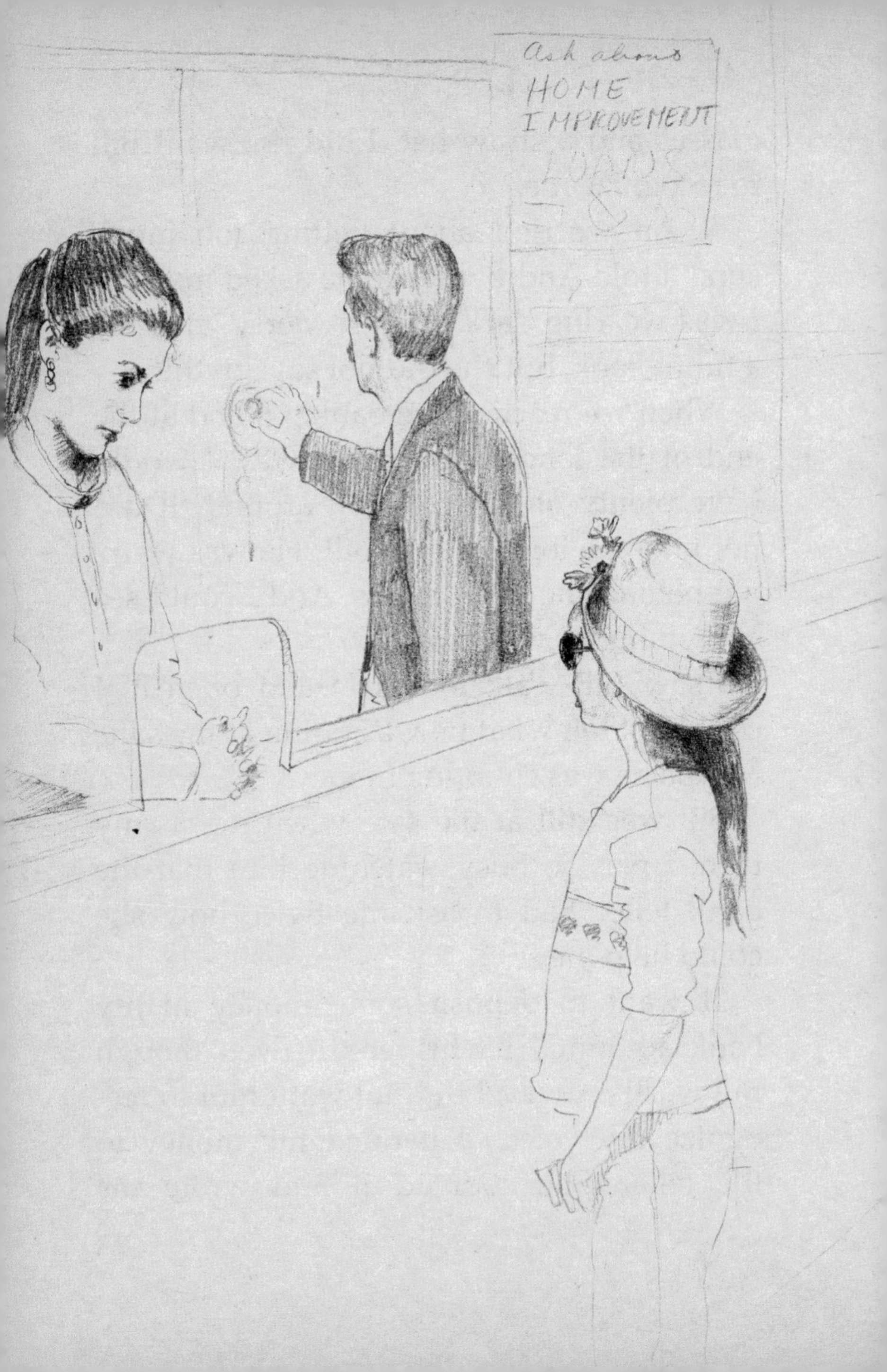
Ask about
HOME
IMPROVEMENT
LOANS

amount on a slip of paper. Then she asked me to sign it. "This is a deposit slip," she explained.

Usually I would be interested in what the teller had to say. But I was so busy watching Bill, I did not pay much attention. The teller had to remind me that it was someone else's turn when I was finished. I hardly heard her. Bill had closed the safe. He announced he was going on his lunch break.

I ran to find Merry and Andrew. They were waiting for me near some big padded armchairs in the lobby. "We have to leave now," I said.

"I am ready," said Andrew. "What took so long?"

I did not answer because Bill was walking out the door. We walked behind him for awhile. Then Andrew stopped to look in the window of a candy store near the bank. Merry and I had to stop too. When Andrew finally turned away, Bill was gone. I was very disappointed.

"What would you like to do downtown?" Merry asked us.

I shrugged. I did not care what we did now.

"I am hungry," Andrew said. "Can we have candy?"

"Why don't we have lunch instead?" Merry suggested.

Andrew wanted to eat at Pizza Express again. (It is near the bank.) Merry and I started to follow him. We walked past a coffee shop. And it is a good thing I looked in the window, because I saw Bill having lunch with the woman in black.

I thought fast. "Please, please can we eat at the coffee shop instead? We have just been to Pizza Express," I said. "It would be good to try something different."

Andrew agreed after Merry told him the coffee shop serves excellent ice cream. For once I did not care about food. I needed to spy on Bill, and catch him in the act — whatever that was.

Lunchtime Spy

Everyone in downtown Stoneybrook seemed to be eating at the coffee shop. Merry, Andrew, and I had to wait for a table. A waitress finally seated us far away from where Bill and his friend were sitting. I had a good view of their table, but I could not hear anything they were saying.

Well . . . I had a good view of the table until the waitress stood in front of it to take someone else's order. (Sigh.) She blocked my view just when Bill was handing something to the woman in black. I stood up to see around the waitress. But I was too late to see what Bill had given his friend.

"Why are you standing up?" Andrew wanted to know.

"Uh," I said, "I just wanted to see the menu better."

"You have a menu right in front of you," Andrew reminded me.

"Right," I said, sitting down. I kept my dark glasses on, just in case. I thought about taking my spy notebook out of my backpack, in case I had to write anything down. But I did not want to explain anything to Merry and Andrew. And Andrew would probably want to read my notebook. I could not let him. It was confidential, until I solved the case. Instead, I just watched Bill and the woman closely. When the waitress was not blocking the table, this is what I saw:

1) THE WOMAN IN BLACK WAS STILL IN BLACK. TODAY SHE WAS WEARING BLACK PANTS AND A BLACK T-SHIRT.

2) BILL ATE A LOT. ALSO, HE SEEMED VERY HAPPY ABOUT SOMETHING.

3) BILL PAID FOR THE MEAL WITH A $100 BILL. (I WAS NOT SITTING TOO FAR AWAY TO SEE THAT.) HE TOOK IT FROM A LARGE WAD OF BILLS HE CARRIED IN HIS POCKET. I COULD NOT BELIEVE IT. I HAD NEVER SEEN THAT MUCH MONEY BEFORE.

"HE JUST PAID WITH A HUNDRED-DOLLAR BILL," I SAID OUT LOUD.

"WHO DID?" ANDREW WANTED TO KNOW.

MERRY TURNED AROUND TO LOOK. "SOME PEOPLE CARRY LARGE AMOUNTS OF CASH AROUND," SHE SAID.

I WONDERED IF BILL HAD STOLEN THAT MONEY FROM THE SAFE.

4) BILL AND HIS FRIEND LEFT BEFORE WE DID. I DECIDED NOT TO FOLLOW THEM OUTSIDE. MERRY PROBABLY WOULD NOT HAVE LET ME. AND MY HAMBURGER AND FRENCH FRIES HAD JUST ARRIVED. EVEN SPIES HAVE TO EAT.

When we came home, I rushed upstairs to record everything I had seen in my spy notebook. Luckily, I remembered a lot. Then

I went to Nancy's house to take care of Pokey. I looked on the kitchen counter for Pokey's medicine. It is always there. But today it was not. Uh-oh. Then I remembered something. I might have left Pokey's medicine in the study. I had left Nancy's house in a big rush the day before.

I carried Pokey upstairs to the study. Sure enough, the medicine was on top of a bunch of papers on the desk. I wondered if Bill had found the medicine. If he had, he would know I had been snooping around. Oh, dear. Did he know what I was doing? Was he waiting to catch me? I was probably the only person who knew what he was up to.

I was feeling more and more nervous. What if Bill were a dangerous criminal? He knew where I lived. He probably even knew my bank account number.

Suddenly I felt very scared. Holding Pokey helped a little. I decided it would be better not to poke around the study anymore. Bill might notice if I moved something.

But as I looked around the study, I got an idea. (A brilliant idea.) I could catch Bill in the act of stealing. And I knew just how to do it.

To Catch a Thief

The next day, I felt fidgety. I tried to play with Andrew, but I could not concentrate. To begin my plan, I had to wait until six P.M., when Bill usually came home from work. My plan was risky. Everything depended on timing.

At five-forty-five I went over to Nancy's house with a blank cassette tape in my backpack.

I let myself inside. I was so scared, I could hear my heart beating. I tried not to think about what Bill would do if he got caught. I rushed upstairs to the study. Then I popped the tape into the stereo, and pressed "play" and "record." Before I left, I opened the blinds at the window.

My tape was 120 minutes long. I hoped Bill would give himself away in the next two hours.

When I left Nancy's house, Bill still wasn't home. (Thank goodness.) He arrived ten minutes later. I know because I was watching from my bedroom window with my binoculars.

Bill turned on the lights in the study. I focused my binoculars. Now I could see a lot. My spy notebook was with me and I recorded everything.

OFFICIAL SPY NOTES CONTINUED
BY SPY KAREN BREWER

6:15 P. M.
I AM WATCHING SUSPECT BILL BARNETT HE IS SITTING AT MR. DAWES'S COMPUTER, TYPING. DARN.

I WISH SOMETHING WOULD HAPPEN, OR THE ONLY
SOUND ON THE TAPE WILL BE TYPING.

6:30 P.M.
NOW SOMETHING IS HAPPENING. THE WOMAN
IN BLACK JUST SHOWED UP. SHE RANG THE DOOR-
BELL, AND BILL WENT DOWNSTAIRS TO LET HER IN.
NOW BOTH OF THEM ARE IN THE STUDY. BILL IS
SITTING AT THE COMPUTER. THE WOMAN IN BLACK
IS LEANING OVER HIS SHOULDER TO SEE THE COM-
PUTER SCREEN. THEY LOOK EXCITED, AND THEY ARE
TALKING. I CANNOT HEAR WHAT THEY ARE SAYING,
OF COURSE. BUT AT LEAST SOMETHING WILL BE
ON THE TAPE.

6:50 P.M.
THE WOMAN IN BLACK JUST PULLED SOMETHING
OUT OF HER BAG. A CALCULATOR? SHE SAT DOWN
AND IS PRESSING THE KEYS ON IT. NOW SHE IS PAT-
TING BILL ON THE BACK. SHE IS GIVING HIM A
HIGH FIVE.
    BILL TURNED AROUND AND IS FACING THE
WINDOW. HE IS POINTING TO THE BLINDS. UH-OH.
CAN HE SEE ME? HE LOOKS ANGRY. HE JUST

84

SAID SOMETHING TO THE WOMAN. SHE SHOOK
HER HEAD, AS IF SHE IS SAYING NO.

QUESTION: IS BILL ASKING HER IF SHE OPENED THE
BLINDS?

NOW BILL IS GETTING OUT OF HIS CHAIR. HE IS
GOING OVER TO THE WINDOW. I AM CROUCHING
DOWN SO HE CANNOT SEE ME.

I PUT MY NOTEBOOK AWAY. WHEN I PEEPED OUT
THE WINDOW AGAIN, THE BLINDS WERE CLOSED.

I TRULY HOPE BILL DID NOT SEE ME. IF HE DID,
I WILL BE IN A LOT OF TROUBLE.

MOMMY CALLED ME THEN. DINNER WAS READY.

I DECIDED TO PHONE HANNIE AFTER DINNER
TO TELL HER WHAT WAS HAPPENING. MAYBE NOW
SHE WOULD BELIEVE ME.

"Hello, Hannie," I said when she picked
up the phone.

"Is this about Bill again?" Hannie wanted
to know. (She did not even say hello.)

"Yes," I said. "But this time I have proof
something is going on."

Before Hannie could answer, I told her the blue light I had seen had been coming from Mr. Dawes's computer when Bill tried to get into the bank's files.

Hannie was quiet so I kept talking. I told her about finding Bill's red notebook and seeing the word *withdrawal* in it.

Hannie whistled.

"Do you believe me now?" I said.

"I am starting to," answered Hannie.

When I finished telling Hannie the story, especially about what I had just seen this afternoon, Hannie apologized. "I should have believed you sooner," she said.

The Secret Password

The next morning I woke up when it was still dark. I looked next door. Bill's car was there, so I knew I could not check the tape yet. I was worried. What if the recorder had not worked? What if Bill had noticed it running?

I went downstairs and made myself breakfast. I had just finished eating when Mommy came downstairs. She looked surprised to see me up so early. "Are you all right, Karen?" she asked.

"I am fine. I just could not sleep."

Mommy frowned and felt my forehead. "I am fine," I repeated.

I checked the time. It was still very early. But I had promised Hannie I would call her when Bill left the house. She wanted to be with me when I snuck in to get the tape, which was good. I felt safer with her there.

Hannie answered on the first ring. She told me she had woken up early too. She had not slept well after I called the night before. She was too excited.

"Has Bill left the house yet?" Hannie wanted to know.

"Yes. He just left. Come over as soon as you can. We will get the tape and bring it back here. We can listen to it on my old tape player." (I did not want to stay long at Nancy's house. What if Bill came back?)

Hannie arrived about twenty minutes later. Mommy and Seth were just leaving for work. Merry was making breakfast for Andrew.

I took Hannie outside. "Oh, Karen, I am

scared. I am scared to go over there," she whispered.

"We will not stay long. You can be the lookout near the front door. I will go inside and get the tape."

Hannie sat on the front steps. She was supposed to yell if Bill or his girlfriend showed up. I went to the back of the house, unlocked the door, and rushed upstairs to the study. The stereo was still on and set to "record." I turned everything off and took out the tape.

Suddenly I heard a soft thump behind me! I spun around, but it was just Pokey. He had jumped onto Mr. Dawes's big padded leather chair.

"Oh, Pokey, you scared me!" I cried. My heart was pounding. "Did you follow me in here?"

"Mew-eek," said Pokey. I stroked his back for a minute, then ran downstairs with the tape.

"I have it!" I shouted to Hannie when I saw her. "Let's go."

We ran all the way to my house and up the stairs to my room. It took us awhile to find my tape player. I finally saw it in the back of my messy closet.

Hannie put in the tape and pressed "play." I turned up the volume. At first we could not hear anything.

"Karen, are you sure you turned on Nancy's recorder?" Hannie asked.

"Of course I did. Bill did not come home right away."

At last we heard the sound of a computer starting up, then lots of typing. The next sound on the tape was a doorbell.

"Soon we will hear people talking," I told Hannie.

I was right. The next thing on the tape was a woman's voice. "How much did you get?"

"Over five thousand this time," Bill's voice said on the tape. I looked at Hannie, who stared back at me.

"Great," we heard the woman say. "We have more than twenty thousand dollars

now. When will anyone at the bank notice?"

"I think we still have a week or so," Bill replied. "The bank sends out its statements at the end of the month. Then people will see that they have less money. But I tried to take from a lot of accounts, just a little from each one. That makes it less noticeable."

"You thought of everything," said the woman. "By the time anyone does find out, we'll be gone."

"I wasted a lot of time looking for that password. I spent days hunting around here for a clue. I did not think I would ever find it."

"Thank goodness for that nosy little kid."

I could hear Bill chuckling on the tape. I could not wait to hear who the nosy kid was. How could anyone around here help Bill find the password? It was a secret.

"She will never know how much she helped us," we heard Bill say.

"What was the password anyway?" the woman wanted to know.

"Percy. The name of the Daweses' old

dog." Bill's voice on the tape was loud and clear.

The tape stopped soon after Bill mentioned me. I could not believe it. I gave Bill the password.

"Karen, we have to give this tape to the police," Hannie cried.

"I will play it for Mommy when she comes home for lunch," I said. "The police will listen to her."

18

A Matter for the Police

Hannie and I rushed downstairs when we heard Mommy come home. "Mommy, you have to listen to this tape," I said. I waved it in front of her.

Mommy looked at me blankly.

Hannie and I were so excited, we both started talking at once. Mommy made us sit down and take turns speaking.

I talked first. I told Mommy about taping Bill and his girlfriend. "Bill really is robbing the bank," Hannie added. "The tape proves it."

Mommy was not happy I had taped Bill and his friend. "That is against the law, Karen," Mommy said. But she agreed to listen to the tape.

I explained that not much happened on the tape until the woman in black arrived. So I fast-forwarded the tape to her part.

"How much did you get?" came the woman's voice. As Bill and the woman kept talking, Mommy just shook her head. She looked kind of pale.

When the tape was over, Mommy closed her eyes for a moment and took a deep breath. "Karen, it was wrong of you to spy. But I see you were right about Bill. I recognize his voice. And I am sorry I doubted you. I will call the police now."

While Mommy was calling, I rewound the tape. (Mommy also called the craft center to tell them she was taking the afternoon off.)

"A detective is coming to the house," Mommy announced. Then she hugged us. "I am glad you found out about this, girls.

But you could have been in danger. What if Bill had caught you in the house?"

I did not want to think about that.

Merry and Andrew came home while we were waiting for the detective. Hannie and I wasted no time telling them about Bill. "Bill is a robber," Andrew said. He looked as if he were going to cry.

Just then the doorbell rang.

Detective Stanton had a deep voice. I was disappointed that he was wearing an ordinary suit instead of a uniform. But at least he was wearing a badge. He talked to Mommy for a long time.

After awhile, Detective Stanton looked at Mommy. "Are you certain this isn't some kind of joke, Mrs. Engle?"

"I am sure," Mommy said.

"My partner and I will interview Mr. Barnett," said Detective Stanton. "But first I will need to go downtown to look at some bank records. In the meantime, please keep a low profile over here."

"What does that mean?" I asked.

"It means we must not interfere any more right now," Mommy answered.

Soon the detective left. And we had to wait a long time for him to come back.

Two days later, Hannie and I were in my room. We saw Bill arrive and go into Nancy's house. Then we saw Detective Stanton and another detective get out of a parked car down the street. (It did not look like a police car, but I guess it was.) They rang Nancy's doorbell. When Bill answered, they talked to him. Then they all went inside.

I looked at Hannie. She looked at me. We were thinking the same thing. Then we did something we probably should not have done. We tiptoed downstairs and slipped out the back door. We sneaked over to Nancy's house and crouched below her living room window. (It was open, except for a screen.)

"And how do you explain this?" I heard Detective Stanton ask. Bill did not answer right away.

Then we heard him say, "Well—we were just kidding around. We . . . Why have you come after me? Has somebody told you I did something wrong?"

I knew that the police would not be able to use my tape to arrest Bill. But they must have found out a lot more about Bill's robbery at the bank!

"We'll ask the questions here," the other man said. "We asked the bank to check their records today. They found a number of unauthorized withdrawals. Now we have a warrant to search this house."

"We plan to search your girlfriend's house too," Detective Stanton said.

"No, no, wait," said Bill. There was a pause. "Okay, look, it's all my fault. Can we keep her out of it if I pay the money back, and explain what happened?"

"Tell us about it. If your story matches the evidence we have, we'll do whatever we can for your friend," said Detective Stanton.

Bill started talking. He and Juliette (his girlfriend) wanted to get married, but her parents would not let them. They needed money to go away by themselves. Bill said it was his idea to break into the bank's computer system and steal from people's accounts. He was talking about how sorry he was when Hannie and I tiptoed away from the window and went back to my house. Luckily nobody had missed us. Bill did sound sorry. But I felt sorrier for all those people Bill stole from. The only good thing about Bill was that at least he wanted to protect his girlfriend, instead of blame her.

I watched from my window as the detectives led Bill out the front door in handcuffs. I never had the chance to ask him if he had stolen money from my account.

Calling Seattle

Hannie and I watched Bill and Detective Stanton drive away. Then we saw the other detective coming toward our house. The doorbell rang. Soon Mommy called us downstairs.

"This is Detective Martinez," Mommy told us. "He says Bill confessed and is under arrest. They are going to pick up his girlfriend too."

"You did very well," Detective Martinez said to me. "Maybe you should consider a career in criminal justice when you are older."

I could not think of what to say. I want to be an actress when I grow up. Could I also be a policewoman? Maybe I could play one on TV.

Before he left, Detective Martinez shook my hand, then Hannie's. We felt like Very Important People.

Seth came home just as Detective Martinez was leaving. He looked surprised to see a police detective in our house. "Did we get robbed?" he asked.

Detective Martinez laughed. "No," he answered. "But Stoneybrook Savings Bank did. Thanks to Karen here, we caught the thief."

Seth raised his eyebrows. Then Detective Martinez and Mommy told him the whole story. "I told you Bill was suspicious," I added, after Mommy finished talking.

"You did," Seth agreed. "I am sorry we did not believe you."

"There is one more thing we have to do,"

said Mommy, after Detective Martinez left.

"Call Nancy's parents," I said.

"Right."

Seth talked to Nancy's parents first. Then Mommy spoke to them.

"Can I talk to Nancy?" I whispered to Mommy while she was on the phone. Mommy nodded and kept talking to Nancy's parents. Finally Mommy handed me the phone.

"Is it Nancy?" I asked.

Mommy shook her head. "Nancy's parents want to talk to you first."

"Hello?" I said when I picked up the phone.

"Hello, Karen. It sounds like you saved the bank from ruin," Mr. Dawes said. "We cannot thank you enough."

"It was nothing," I said modestly. Then I told Nancy's parents I was sorry I gave Bill the password by accident.

"There is no need to apologize," said Mr. Dawes. "You did not know what he was up to."

I also pointed out that I had done a good job as a house-sitter, even though I was not the one they hired.

"You did an excellent job, Karen," said Mrs. Dawes.

"You certainly did," Mr. Dawes agreed.

"I know it is not nice to spy on people," I said. "But in this case, wasn't it for the best?"

The Daweses laughed. Then Nancy came to the phone. We talked for a long time. I did not tell her the whole story about Bill. Her parents could do that. But she already knew I had saved the bank. "I also took very good care of Pokey and your house," I said.

Then Nancy told me the best news of all. Her family was coming home early. In fact, they were leaving tomorrow. Hannie and I could not wait to see Nancy again.

Congratulations to the Ace Detective

"This is a colobus," said Nancy. She held up a picture of a black-and-white monkey with a bushy white tail.

"It is so cute," squealed Hannie.

"I like the baby gorillas," I said, pointing to another picture.

"They were the most fun animals in the zoo," Nancy said.

Hannie, Nancy, and I were in Nancy's room looking at her pictures of Seattle. (Most of the pictures were of the animals in the Seattle Zoo.) "It was the best zoo I have ever been to," Nancy told us.

We were waiting for Mr. Dawes to come home. He was going to take us to his bank. He said he had a surprise planned for me. I could not wait to see what it was.

"Girls, are you ready?" Mr. Dawes called from downstairs. We had not heard him come in the house.

"Yes, we are coming!" Nancy shouted back. She stood up and smoothed out her pink skirt. She was all dressed up. So was I. Mommy had told me this trip to the bank would be special.

On the way, I asked about the surprise. But still no one would tell me anything.

I walked inside the bank with Mr. Dawes, Hannie, and Nancy. "She's here!" someone shouted. Then a whole bunch of people crowded around us and started clapping.

"That applause is for you, Karen," Mr. Dawes told me.

For me? I stared at all the people smiling at me, and bowed. (I love applause.)

"Now for the real surprise," said Mr. Dawes. He led me to a table that was decorated with pink crepe paper and pink roses. (Pink is my favorite color.) Then he picked up the envelope that lay on the table and handed it to me.

"This is a check for you, Karen," said Mr. Dawes. "It is our way of thanking you for saving the bank."

I wanted to deposit the check into my bank account right away. But first I had to make sure my account was safe.

"Did Bill steal from my account?" I asked.

"No, he did not," answered Mr. Dawes. (That was a relief.)

"Bill is returning the stolen money to the accounts he robbed," Nancy added.

"Good," I said.

Before we left, I deposited my check. This time I did not even have to wait in line for a teller. I felt like a Gigundoly Important Person.

"Next stop, the craft center," said Mr. Dawes.

Hannie, Nancy, and I spent the rest of the afternoon helping Mommy sell her bracelets. We also helped sell necklaces and earrings. Everyone loved Mommy's bracelets. She sold almost everything she had made.

When the fair was over, Mommy gave Hannie, Nancy, and me little bracelets she had made just for us. I loved my silver bracelet with the turquoise in it. I put it on right away. Having two jobs was not bad at all.

L. GODWIN

About the Author

ANN M. MARTIN lives in New York City and loves animals, especially cats. She has two cats of her own, Gussie and Woody.

Other books by Ann M. Martin that you might enjoy are *Stage Fright*; *Me and Katie (the Pest)*; and the books in *The Baby-sitters Club* series.

Ann likes ice cream and *I Love Lucy*. And she has her own little sister, whose name is Jane.

Little Sister

Don't miss #112

KAREN'S NEW HOLIDAY

I liked being in charge of the group. I explained about seeing the *Kid Power!* show and how we could make a difference. "We can make a national holiday for August," I said. I opened my new yellow notebook to the first page. It was my official national holiday notebook. "Does anyone have any ideas for the holiday?" I asked. I was all ready to take notes.

"Can there be trick-or-treating on this new holiday?" Andrew asked. "I love getting candy."

"And dressing up," Melody added. "I love wearing costumes."

David Michael stopped tossing the soccer ball in the air. "I think we should get lots of presents, like on Christmas."

"Let's have a parade and lots of food, like on Thanksgiving!" Maria said, jumping up and down.

I was having a hard time writing all the ideas down.

Little Sister

by Ann M. Martin
author of The Baby-sitters Club®

More Titles... ➡

❑ MQ69188-0 #80	Karen's Christmas Tree	$2.99
❑ MQ69189-9 #81	Karen's Accident	$2.99
❑ MQ69190-2 #82	Karen's Secret Valentine	$3.50
❑ MQ69191-0 #83	Karen's Bunny	$3.50
❑ MQ69192-9 #84	Karen's Big Job	$3.50
❑ MQ69193-7 #85	Karen's Treasure	$3.50
❑ MQ69194-5 #86	Karen's Telephone Trouble	$3.50
❑ MQ06585-8 #87	Karen's Pony Camp	$3.50
❑ MQ06586-6 #88	Karen's Puppet Show	$3.50
❑ MQ06587-4 #89	Karen's Unicorn	$3.50
❑ MQ06588-2 #90	Karen's Haunted House	$3.50
❑ MQ06589-0 #91	Karen's Pilgrim	$3.50
❑ MQ06590-4 #92	Karen's Sleigh Ride	$3.50
❑ MQ06591-2 #93	Karen's Cooking Contest	$3.50
❑ MQ06592-0 #94	Karen's Snow Princess	$3.50
❑ MQ06593-9 #95	Karen's Promise	$3.50
❑ MQ06594-7 #96	Karen's Big Move	$3.50
❑ MQ06595-5 #97	Karen's Paper Route	$3.50
❑ MQ06596-3 #98	Karen's Fishing Trip	$3.50
❑ MQ49760-X #99	Karen's Big City Mystery	$3.50
❑ MQ50051-1 #100	Karen's Book	$3.50
❑ MQ50053-8 #101	Karen's Chain Letter	$3.50
❑ MQ50054-6 #102	Karen's Black Cat	$3.50
❑ MQ50055-4 #103	Karen's Movie Star	$3.99
❑ MQ50056-2 #104	Karen's Christmas Carol	$3.99
❑ MQ50057-0 #105	Karen's Nanny	$3.99
❑ MQ50058-9 #106	Karen's President	$3.99
❑ MQ50059-7 #107	Karen's Copycat	$3.99
❑ MQ43647-3	Karen's Wish Super Special #1	$3.25
❑ MQ44834-X	Karen's Plane Trip Super Special #2	$3.25
❑ MQ44827-7	Karen's Mystery Super Special #3	$3.25
❑ MQ45644-X	Karen, Hannie, and Nancy The Three Musketeers Super Special #4	$2.95
❑ MQ45649-0	Karen's Baby Super Special #5	$3.50
❑ MQ46911-8	Karen's Campout Super Special #6	$3.25
❑ MQ55407-7	BSLS Jump Rope Pack	$5.99
❑ MQ73914-X	BSLS Playground Games Pack	$5.99
❑ MQ89735-7	BSLS Photo Scrapbook Book and Camera Pack	$9.99
❑ MQ47677-7	BSLS School Scrapbook	$2.95
❑ MQ13801-4	Baby-sitters Little Sister Laugh Pack	$6.99
❑ MQ26497-2	Karen's Summer Fill-In Book	$2.95

Available wherever you buy books, or use this order form.

Scholastic Inc., P.O. Box 7502, Jefferson City, MO 65102

Please send me the books I have checked above. I am enclosing $_____
(please add $2.00 to cover shipping and handling). Send check or money order – no cash or C.O.Ds please.

Name_____Birthdate_____

Address_____

City_____State/Zip_____

Please allow four to six weeks for delivery. Offer good in U.S.A. only. Sorry, mail orders are not available to residents of Canada. Prices subject to change.   BSLS998

LITTLE 🍎 APPLE®

Here are some of our favorite Little Apples.

Once you take a bite out of a Little Apple book—you'll want to read more!

Books for Kids with BIG Appetites!

❑ NA45899-X **Amber Brown Is Not a Crayon**
    Paula Danziger **$2.99**

❑ NA42833-0 **Catwings** Ursula K. LeGuin **$3.50**

❑ NA42832-2 **Catwings Return** Ursula K. LeGuin **$3.50**

❑ NA41821-1 **Class Clown** Johanna Hurwitz **$3.50**

❑ NA42400-9 **Five True Horse Stories** Margaret Davidson **$3.50**

❑ NA42401-7 **Five True Dog Stories** Margaret Davidson **$3.50**

❑ NA43868-9 **The Haunting of Grade Three**
    Grace Maccarone **$3.50**

❑ NA40966-2 **Rent a Third Grader** B.B. Hiller **$3.50**

❑ NA41944-7 **The Return of the Third Grade Ghost Hunters**
    Grace Maccarone **$2.99**

❑ NA47463-4 **Second Grade Friends** Miriam Cohen **$3.50**

❑ NA45729-2 **Striped Ice Cream** Joan M. Lexau **$3.50**